Gardiner Greene Hubbard, Mabel Gardiner Hubbard Bell

The Story of the Rise of the Oral Method in America

I0692635

Gardiner Greene Hubbard, Mabel Gardiner Hubbard Bell

The Story of the Rise of the Oral Method in America

ISBN/EAN: 9783337330019

Printed in Europe, USA, Canada, Australia, Japan

Cover: Foto ©Andreas Hilbeck / pixelio.de

More available books at **www.hansebooks.com**

THE STORY

OF THE

RISE OF THE ORAL METHOD

IN AMERICA

AS TOLD IN THE WRITINGS
OF THE LATE

HON. GARDINER G. HUBBARD

WASHINGTON, D. C.
PRESS OF W. F. ROBERTS
1898

INTRODUCTION

AT this meeting of the National Educational Association now being held in the National Capital, teachers of the deaf, for the first time, appear as an organized body forming an integral part of the Association. This affiliation of teachers of the deaf with teachers of the hearing comes about so naturally in 1898, and is such a logical consequence of all recent work for the deaf, that little comment has been excited, and perhaps few among the younger teachers realize what an advance this event marks in the history of the deaf, what a change it exemplifies in the public regard towards this class. Yet it is an event that challenges the attention, not only of friends of the deaf, but of all observers of humanitarian progress. It marks the dying out of the old popular prejudices against the deaf as a peculiar people, for whose instruction strange and mysterious methods must be employed. It marks the dawn of a new era when the deaf person shall be regarded as capable of the same kind and degree of education as any other American, and the methods used in his instruction approximate more nearly to those employed by ordinary teachers. Thirty years ago, such a *rapprochement* as has taken place would have seemed beyond the range of possibility, so opposed were the methods considered necessary in which to convey knowledge to the deaf. Ninety years ago it was doubted if they could be educated at all; whether they could even be considered as within the pale of the law. Now, they are preparing to enter our colleges and universities for the hearing.

Indeed the long life of one man may well have witnessed the lifting up of the deaf as a class from the lowest to well nigh the highest plane of civilization. With this great achievement—great even in this wonderful century of humanitarian accomplishment,—will forever be associated the name of my father, the late Honorable Gardiner Greene Hubbard of Washington, D. C.

His attention was first called to this subject in 1862. At that time, the deaf were truly dumb—extraordinary beings whose sometimes graceful, more often uncouth gestures and facial contortions

4

made them in public places objects of curiosity, sometimes of pity, at others of ridicule; always things strange and apart. I well remember my own feelings of awe, not unmixed with horror, when I first saw some of these strange people. I was then a little deaf child myself, between whom and the inevitable doom of becoming like these, there stood nothing but a father's courage and determination and a mother's infinite love and patience. But for these, my fate had been sealed, for there was not one school where children could have been taught except through signs. No one believed in articulation then. Teachers of the deaf, long accustomed to signs, extolled their beauty and the ease and rapidity with which they and others proficient in their use were enabled by this means to communicate with the deaf. Satisfied with giving their pupils a good common school education, and the ability to read and write English as well as the generality of foreigners, they could not realize the importance of furnishing them with many and ready means of intercourse with their neighbors, of making English the mother tongue in which they should habitually think as well as read and write, and of making them as precisely as possible like other people.

There was, at this time, in Massachusetts, no school for the deaf of any kind at all. My father determined that there should be one, and he himself undertook to establish it. The other schools of the country, with one exception,* were known as "Asylums" or "Institutions." His should be known specifically as a "school." The others were for "deaf-mutes" or "deaf and dumb." His should be for "deaf" as well as "deaf-mute" children. The others rarely admitted pupils under 12 or 14 years. His should take them from five to ten. The others employed men principally as teachers. His should make large use of women as better fitted to teach the very young. The others pursued the "manual" or "sign" method of instruction, which excluded articulation. His should employ the "Oral" or "Articulation" method, which excluded signs.

In March, 1864, he prepared a petition to the Massachusetts Legislature for an Act of Incorporation creating himself and a few others a Body Corporate "by the name of the Massachusetts *School* for deaf-mutes, for the purpose of training and educating *deaf* and deaf-mute children," etc. The bill was presented to the Legislature March 16, 1864, by Mr. Robert Johnson, member from Dorchester, and referred to the Committee on Public Charitable Institutions, and the new movement soon became widely

*The Tennessee school.

6

known through the public press. The petition was opposed before the Committee by representatives of the American Asylum for Deaf Mutes at Hartford, Conn., and in this way was inaugurated the memorable controversy over the merits of the Sign and Oral methods of instructing the deaf, which culminated in 1867 with the establishment of the Clarke Institution at Northampton, Mass.—as an oral school—with Mr. Hubbard as its first president.

It is interesting to note that the continuous progress of the oral movement since then has brought about the gradual abandonment of the word "mute" or "dumb" as applied to deaf children, and the word "asylum" as applied to their schools. It has also led to a very general lowering of the age of admission ; the establishment of infant schools and day schools for the deaf, and the employment of women as teachers for the young. We now have 95 schools with 9,749 pupils ; 5,498 receive instruction in articulation, and of these, 3,466 are taught wholly or chiefly by the Oral method without the use of Signs.

These schools give occupation to 1,188 instructors, including 260 industrial teachers employed in workshops, etc., for teaching trades and occupations to the deaf. Deducting the 260 industrial or trade instructors from the grand total, we find that Articulation teachers now form the majority of the actual teaching force employed—487 articulation teachers to 441 other teachers, including the superintendents and principals of the schools themselves.

Is not this a grand result to have been largely instrumental in bringing to pass in the space of thirty-five years?

But this is not all. The standard of instruction has been raised all along the line, and now orally taught pupils are prepared for admission into ordinary high schools and academies from which they are preparing to enter our colleges and universities along with hearing young men and women. Dr. Caroline A. Yale, the principal of the Clarke school —the school which arose from my father's efforts, and of which he was president for the first ten years —reports that three of its graduates, after having passed through the high school, are preparing to enter the Lawrence Scientific School; another is in the third year in the Columbia School of Mines, a fifth is in the Colby Academy. She says further that the standing of all the pupils is high, in some cases marvelously high, and that all but one were born deaf—that is, they are of the class which Mr. Turner said could never be taught articulation.

Mr. Turner was one of the early Principals of the American School at Hartford, Conn. (then the

American "Asylum"), and in 1867 he appeared before the Joint Special Committee of the Massachusetts Legislature and took part in the closing scenes of the great controversy concerning speech for the deaf, and said :

> "The attempt to teach articulation has never been a part of the regular system of instruction of the deaf and dumb, and I hope never will be. We can give them a measure of vocalization, imperfect, to be sure, we can teach some of them to pronounce, parrot-like, words something in the way we do, but we cannot make them (the deaf-born) understand the use of vocal language, with its articulation, its emphasis, its point. It has never been done ; it never can be done."

Contrast this with the following extract from the 1898 Report of Mr. Job Williams, the present principal of the American School:

> "The aim of all school instruction should be to aid the pupil to master the English language in order that he may have easy communication with the hearing world about him through the English language, by spoken English in all cases where possible, but when that proves impossible, by written or spelled English."
> "Even a small degree of speech is valuable. Teach speech, speech, speech by all means, and to the fullest degree, and use it whenever practicable, in school and out of school. Encourage it at all times, and let non-English means of communication be discouraged

9

wherever the English language will answer equally well. English either spoken, written or spelled, is, in the main, the .language of our school exercises."

No stronger testimony could be given to the immense change of sentiment that has taken place among the teachers of the deaf since that time, thirty-five years ago, when my father went from school to school, in vain seeking where he might get help and encouragement in teaching articulation to his little girl suddenly bereft of hearing. It is through forces and agencies set in motion by his initiative, encouraged by his indomitable will, and guided in momentous crises by his wise judgment, that this great change has taken place, and that here in Washington at the meeting of the National Educational Association will be assembled teachers of the deaf. To many who visit the National Educational Association, the whole subject of the instruction of the deaf will be entirely new. Some may never have met a completely deaf person—one of the class miscalled "deaf and dumb." To others it may be a matter of surprise that some of the deaf have been taught to speak so well that only peculiarities of voice and pronunciation betray lack of hearing. To all, the subject cannot fail to be interesting—so interesting that the question must arise— How did all this come about? What were the agencies that produced these wonderful results? It is the purpose of this little book to answer these questions, and to answer them in Mr. Hubbard's words, the words of one who, as Miss Yale so beautifully says :—

> " In his own little child's voice heard the prophecy that deaf children might speak, and to whom is due probably more than to any other one man, the fact that all America has realized the fulfillment of that prophecy."

> MABEL GARDINER BELL.

TWIN OAKS, WASHINGTON, D. C.,
July 9, 1898.

NOTE—The story as told in this little book is gathered chiefly from Mr. Hubbard's writings. It has occasionally been found necessary to make some changes in the phraseology in order to make a connected story from the different publications, but these changes have been few and unimportant. Some additions have been made where they seemed to strengthen or elucidate Mr. Hubbard's story. All statements of facts within Mr. Hubbard's personal knowledge and all opinions expressed by him are given in his own words.

THE STORY OF THE RISE OF THE
ORAL METHOD.

A LL great movements start from a small center.
Our broadest charities have grown from some
individual human need. My own interest in
the education of the deaf and my earnest efforts to
introduce what I believed to be a better method of
instruction than the one then in use, sprang from my
anxiety for my little deaf child. If therefore, in this
brief review of deaf mute education in this country,
my narrative becomes somewhat personal, may I be
excused?

There have been many isolated and more or less
successful attempts to teach deaf persons to speak in
Europe and even in America previous to 1700:—but
it was not until the latter part of the eighteenth
century that systematic efforts were made in Europe
to gather deaf children into special schools devoted
to their instruction. The establishment of schools
for the deaf was attempted in this country very early

in this century by Francis Green in Massachusetts, and Colonel Bolling in Virginia, both fathers of deaf children. Neither effort however was crowned with success, so that when in 1816 the parents and friends of a little deaf girl in Hartford, Connecticut, sought for her some means of instruction, it was found that there were no schools for the deaf in America. This little girl was Alice Coggswell, daughter of Dr. Coggswell, a prominent citizen of Hartford. Her situation excited the sympathy of many friends and led to inquiries as to the number of deaf mutes in this country. To the surprise of all there were found to be about four hundred in New England and about two thousand in the whole United States. It was at once determined to found an institution for the instruction of this hitherto neglected class and to send the Rev. Thomas Hopkins Gallaudet abroad to ascertain what had been done and what were the best modes of instruction. Mr. Gallaudet was at this time a young minister just ready to enter upon his profession. He was a friend and neighbor of Dr. Coggswell and much interested in Alice; and one of the best men probably that ever lived, but as was said by one of his oldest friends "a good and singularly useful rather than a great man, somewhat deficient in boldness and originality." He sailed for England in May, 1815, and on his arrival in London hastened to Dr. Watson's school where the system then taught was articulation. He applied for admission in order to learn this system, but was refused. He then went to Edinburgh, where another articulation school was in operation. Here he met with new obstacles from the obligation which had been imposed upon the institution in that city not to instruct teachers in the art for a term of years.

Mr. Gallaudet was thus thwarted in his plans, and the system of articulation lost to this country for a generation. After these repeated disappointments and discouragements Mr. Gallaudet had recourse to the Abbe Sicard of Paris—successor and pupil of the Abbe De l'Epee—whom he had met in London. The Abbe welcomed him most cordially, admitted him into his school without any conditions, and gave him every facility for learning the system of teaching deaf mutes invented by the Abbe De l'Epee. It was therefore by accident entirely, or as Mr. Gallaudet himself considered it, by the hand of Providence, that he went to France and finally returned to America bringing with him the French system of signs, with its peculiar idioms of construction, instead of the English method of articulation.

During his absence in 1816, an act of incorporation was granted to the "Connecticut Asylum" at Hartford, Conn., and subscriptions were asked to this new charity, "its views having nothing of a local kind." This institution was opened with seven pupils, April 15, 1817. In the year 1819 Congress gave the Asylum a grant of land, and its name was changed to the "American Asylum," and pupils from all States were admitted on equal terms.

The New York Institution was opened in May, 1818, and other schools in different States from time to time. All these schools were conducted on the same system as that pursued at Hartford, and were taught by teachers who had been trained there, and who, with great fidelity, carried on a uniform system of instruction. In 1860, there were in operation twenty-two schools for the deaf in the United States, with 2,000 scholars. This system which was used in all our schools was the French, and is a language of signs or pantomime, called by its teachers the natural language of the deaf-mute. The manual alphabet, or the spelling of words upon the fingers, was used to some extent, but pantomime was the chief medium of communication. The time of instruction was generally six years, commencing at about twelve years of age.

Articulation was not taught in these schools. It was stated at the very founding of the American Asylum that articulation would form no part of the course of instruction, and that the teachers would "not waste their labor and that of their pupils upon this comparatively useless branch of education."*

We gratefully acknowledge that great and good results were accomplished by the deaf mute schools in this country. Thousands were instructed, not only in the various branches of education, but in many mechanical arts. So that instead of being a burden to the States or to their friends they can support themselves and families and amply repay the cost of their own education. But in our midst was growing up a distinct race, using what is called in one of the reports of the New York Institution a "pantomimic dialect," a language of their own,

---

* Third Report American Asylum for 1819, p. 7.

unknown to their friends, without literature, and though, perhaps, often beautiful and expressive, still vague and indefinite. Vague reports were occasionally brought to this country of the system used in Germany where the deaf were taught to speak and read from the lips; but from the time that Mr. Gallaudet went abroad, in 1815, until the year 1844 no teacher of the deaf and dumb ever visited Europe or made any inquiries into the system of articulation. For a generation our institutions pursued one system without any accurate knowledge of other methods.

In 1843, Horace Mann, then Secretary of the Board of Education of Massachusetts, in company with Dr. Howe traveled through Europe and visited some of the European institutions for deaf mutes. In his Seventh Report he gave a short account of the system of education adopted in the German schools, and strongly advocated that system as superior to the one in use in our own country.

Horace Mann and Dr. S. G. Howe, co-workers in many benevolent efforts, were the ablest friends the deaf mutes had in Massachusetts. The attention of Dr. Howe was especially directed to the subject of deaf-mute education, through his interest in two deaf, dumb and blind pupils,—Laura Bridgman and Oliver Caswell,—who were taught with great success, from 1837 to 1845, by the finger alphabet; while Julia Brice, also deaf, dumb and blind, was taught for many years at Hartford by signs, with little success.

Mr. Mann's report excited such general interest

that the American Asylum at Hartford and the New York Institution for Deaf Mutes, sent gentlemen abroad carefully to examine and study these systems. They returned, and reported that the system adopted in this country produced better results than those obtained abroad, and therefore advised that no fundamental change be made.

Mr. Weld, of the American Asylum, recommended that greater attention be paid to teaching articulation to semi-mute and semi-deaf pupils. In accordance with his suggestion, articulation was taught at the Asylum, by a teacher employed for that purpose. These efforts to engraft the German system of articulation upon the French system of signs, then in use in our country, proved a failure ; and were gradually abandoned.

They failed, as they always will fail if attempted in a school, where the sign language is the vernacular. A fair trial can only be made where articulation and reading from the lips form the only medium of communication taught, and the only one allowed. The two cannot be carried on together. The language of signs is without doubt more attractive to the deaf mute, and will be the language of his life if he is encouraged in its use. If the trial is to be made, if experiment is to be fairly and honestly tested, it must be in schools established for that purpose, and under teachers earnestly and heartily engaged in the work, and at least hopeful of success.

But the labors of Dr. Howe and Mr. Mann were not fruitless. From time to time the attention of the public was called to the subject ; and a few parents whose children had lost their hearing were encouraged by Dr. Howe to persevering efforts to retain the articulation of their children, and teach them to read from the lips.

In 1862 my little girl lost her hearing through a fearful illness; she was a bright, intelligent child of four years, but her language was lisping and imperfect. She could talk a little; she did not know all the letters, though she knew most of them. We had never thought it worth while to hurry her education, as we have that of our younger children. When convinced of her deafness, our great anxiety was to retain her language, and to know how we might carry on her education. We asked the advice of one of the oldest teachers of the deaf. "You can do nothing," was the answer; "when she is ten years old, send her to an institution, where she will be taught the sign language." "But she still speaks; can we not retain her language?" "She will lose it in three months, and become dumb as well as deaf; you cannot retain it." The only teacher of the deaf who gave us the slightest encouragement said that even if her articulation was retained, it would be so imperfect and disagreeable as to be absolutely painful, and that we should not want to hear her talk. We asked if articulation was not taught abroad. "Oh, yes; but then it is not equal to the language of signs." So strong at that time was the feeling in favor of the sign language that when some time later we met Mr. Gallaudet with our little girl, and she spoke to him, he said, with a sigh of regret, "But she will lose the beautiful language of signs."

As I have said, the feeling of all persons who knew anything about deaf mutes was to discourage us from undertaking to teach our little girl articulation. She, herself, was at first unwilling to speak. If she had not been forced to speak, she would soon have lost the power entirely.

It was in this time of our discouragement that we heard of the visit of Mr. Horace Mann and Dr. Howe to the schools of Germany, and their report in favor of the oral system. We turned to Dr. Howe for help. He told us that even children born deaf could be taught to speak, and encouraged us to talk to our little girl and to teach her to recognize the spoken words of our lips. He warned us not to use nor to allow any signs, and never to understand them. Cheered by his encouragement, we groped our way. We knew no signs, not even the manual alphabet ; and there is not a single member of my family who knows the manual alphabet to-day. Our little girl did not know it. She was forced, therefore, to resort to articulation if she would know anything. Gradually light dawned. The child began to recall words forgotten in her long illness, and to add new words to her vocabulary, learned from our lips. A young teacher, Miss Mary H. True, who has ever since been devoted to the instruction of the deaf, but who was then totally inexperienced, though admirably fitted by nature and training for the work, came to our aid. Our little girl joined her sisters in their work and in their play. She spoke imperfectly but intelligibly, and understood those around her. Under Miss True's intelligent teaching, her mental development progressed rapidly and her language grew daily. In 1867, four years after she had lost her hearing, a teacher of one of the ordinary schools of Cambridge, Mass., wrote me: "I have been exceedingly interested in examining the little Mabel, and I am happy to say that she will compare very favorably with children of her own age, and is somewhat in advance of the average of those of ten years (Mabel was nine) who have come under my instruction. I am surprised at the readiness with which she reads from the lips, as I have never talked with her before, and she understood the questions without difficulty." It was in after years that my daughter told me she did not then know that she differed in any way from other children, and sometimes wondered why strangers addressed her younger sisters rather than herself.

We could not but feel that we had chosen the better system of education for our child. Assured of the importance of the early education of a deaf child, as well as the advantages of articulation and lip reading, anxious that the system should be fairly tried for the benefit of other deaf children, and satisfied that this could not be done in schools and with teachers who thoroughly believed in sign language as the only effectual means of instruction for the deaf, I presented a petition to the Legislature of Massachusetts in March, 1864, *praying for a charter

---

*At this time my father and mother's faith in the possibility that their child would sometime speak and read the

23

and an appropriation for a new institution for the instruction of those too young to be received at Hartford, and for those who could hear a little or had once spoken. This was, I believe, the first attempt to establish a school for the purpose of teaching the deaf to speak and read from the lips in the United States. The application was seconded by Dr. Howe, but opposed by Messrs. Stone and Keep, of the American Asylum, on the ground "that the logic of facts was entirely against the system of articulation," and that "the instruction of the deaf by articulation was a theory of visionary enthusiasts, which has been repeatedly tried and abandoned as impracticable." Hon. Lewis J. Dudley of Northampton, a member of the Legislature, had a daughter born deaf, then a pupil in the American Asylum. He was convinced from his observation that it was impossible to teach the deaf to speak, and through his influence our efforts were defeated. The petition had been referred to the Committee on Public Charitable Institutions.

---

lips well enough for her acquirements to be of great use to herself and her friends must have been great indeed, for, writing at a later period, my father admitted that he was afraid to take her before the Committee on Charitable Institutions, to which had been referred his petition of 1864. He says:

"We feared that if we brought her the Committee would say : 'Is that all you have done? Can't she articulate any better than that? We cannot understand a word she says. She cannot read from the lips, and she does not apparently know anything.' We were afraid it would be a complete failure, and that what she had done then would demonstrate the want of success of our plan, and therefore we did not dare to bring her. But still, we knew then that she would improve, that she would learn."—Testimony before Committee of 1867.

24

In their report, dated May 11, 1864, the Committee said:

"We are aware that the two methods of teaching here, called the French and German methods, have their warm friends and advocates. At present the Asylum at Hartford is, as it has always been, an exponent of the French method; that is, teaching by a language of signs and the finger alphabet. The teachers there have not ignored entirely the German method, that is, teaching by the finger alphabet, learning to read words by the motions of the lips and actual articulation by the heretofore mutes.

"Which of these methods is the true one we are not able to say. There was evidence before us demonstrating the advantages of the German method when it succeeded in educating well a semi-mute or mute over that of the French; still it appeared also in evidence that in the earlier stages of education it presented almost insuperable difficulties. Still, difficulty has a charm to a resolute soul. No great prize should cease to be attractive because there are difficulties in the way of its attainment; hence we are satisfied the German method is worthy a long continued and most thorough experiment.

"We were not prepared to recommend an appropriation in answer to the petitions of those interested in a school here taught by the German method.

"The present condition of our State finances did not warrant the expense of such an experiment, and yet we hope private benevolence here will prosecute it, and we would respectfully suggest to the Trustees at Hartford that a still farther and more thorough trial of this method might, under their hands, be more *successful*, or at least forever settle the comparative merits of these different systems of teaching the deaf and dumb. The object is worthy the effort, as restoring to society and all the enjoyments of social life those whom Providence has bereft of a sense of hearing and the power of speech."*

Mrs. Edwin Lamson of Boston, formerly a teacher at the Blind Asylum of Laura Bridgman and Oliver Caswell, who were both blind and deaf, was present at the hearing. Mrs. Lamson gave her evidence against the use of signs in the instruction of the deaf, and in favor of the manual alphabet and the experiment of teaching articulation. The attention of Mrs. Cushing of Boston, who had a deaf daughter, was attracted by the discussion, and, after

---

* My husband says:

"With such a recommendation Mr. Hubbard's bill of 1864 failed to pass the legislature. But great interest had been excited and Mr. Hubbard carried the discussion from the committee to the public, with the object of moulding public opinion and enlisting the aid of individuals in starting an oral school by private means, which might ultimately, if successful, be adopted by the State. In all this he was successful. In 1864 he arranged for discussion of the subject in private houses in Boston, to which were invited a select company of prominent and influential ladies and gentlemen.

"Then Mrs. Cushing became interested and sought for some one to teach articulation to her deaf daughter Fanny. Then Miss Harriet B. Rogers appeared and made the experiment. Then Mr. Hubbard helped her to nurse this one little pupil into a school. He induced men, well-known and trusted by the whole community, to examine the child and certify to the reality of the results attained. This certificate he published in the daily newspapers together with an advertisement asking for pupils. When these were found he raised funds by private subscription and supported Miss Rogers' school at Chelmsford until 1867, when it was removed to Northampton to form the nucleus for the Clarke Institution."

careful consideration, she determined that her child should be taught articulation.*

By the advice of Mrs. Lamson, Mrs. Cushing applied to Miss Rogers, then known as a skillful teacher of speaking children, who, with some hesitation, undertook the task.

A few months of earnest effort convinced Miss Rogers of the great advantages of this system, and so enlisted her sympathies and energies that she determined to devote her life to the work, if a suitable number of pupils could be secured and means to support a school provided.†

In 1865 a meeting was called at the house of Mrs. Lamson in Boston, at which Miss Rogers explained what had already been accomplished and her plans for the future. A sum sufficient to defray the expenses of the undertaking was subscribed by several

---

* In an interview lately, Mrs. Lamson said that my father arranged for a meeting at her house of the Committee and prominent gentlemen and ladies, during which she and Mr. Dudley should discuss the question of the different methods of instruction of the deaf. Mrs. Cushing having called to see Mr. Dudley about her little deaf child. he brought her with him to listen to the discussion. At its conclusion she decided that her daughter should not be taught by signs, and applied to Mrs. Lamson for help.

† Miss Rogers writes recently : "I wanted to get more pupils, and told Mrs. Lamson that I was about discouraged because I could not find any one to help me. Then she said she thought she knew of some one who would be interested, and she spoke of Mr. Hubbard. Mr. Hubbard told her to let him know the next time Miss Rogers came to Boston with her child. I wrote Mrs. Lamson when I would be at her house, supposing I should only see Mr. Hubbard. I had never met him previous to this time. But when I reached the house I found Mr. Hubbard had invited half a dozen more gentlemen—prominent gentlemen—to see the

gentlemen, and in November, 1865, the following advertisement was published:

"Miss Rogers proposes to take a few deaf-mutes as pupils for instruction in articulation and reading from the lips, without the use of signs or the finger alphabet. The number is limited to seven, two of whom are already engaged."

In June, 1866, she opened her school at Chelmsford, with five scholars. Another entered in September and two more in the spring of 1867, and at the expiration of one year she had obtained the desired number of pupils. The success attending these efforts having proved that it was not a visionary scheme, but a practical work; its friends determined to make a second application to the Legislature. Dr. S. G. Howe, the Chairman of the Board of State Charities and F. B. Sanborn, Esq., Secretary, also advocated an improved system of instruction in their second and third annual reports, 1866 and 1867, and recommended that the education of the deaf should be commenced at an earlier age, continued for a longer period, and that schools should be provided for the deaf within the limits of the State.

---

child and see what had been done. Among them was the Rev. Thomas Hill, President of Harvard College, and Rev. Dr Kirk.

"At the close of the meeting Rev. Dr. Kirk drew up the certificate and the other gentlemen signed it. Mr. Hubbard took that certificate and wrote the advertisement and had it inserted in the Boston and Providence papers.

"Mr. Hubbard, from the very first time that I saw him, was always helping me in every way possible. From that very first interview he aided me in every way. I could not have opened the school in Chelmsford without him."

In the Autumn of 1866, Mr. Talbot then Lieut.-Governor of Massachusetts and myself called on Governor Bullock and asked him, in his message to the Legislature, to refer to our school and favor an application we intended to make for a charter for it. To our great surprise and pleasure he told us that he had that morning received a letter from a gentleman in Northampton offering $50,000 if a school for the deaf could be established in Northampton. The name of the gentleman, Mr. Clarke, was not then given to us. Mr. Clarke himself had no knowledge of the school at Chelmsford, but for some years he had felt the importance of a school for the deaf in Massachusetts. His interest in the subject was probably first aroused by his own deafness and was strengthened by his acquaintance with Miss Dudley, the daughter of Hon. Lewis J. Dudley of Northampton, His friends conferred with Governor Bullock, who cordially entered into Mr. Clarke's views and, in these eloquent words, laid the matter before the Legislature in his message of January, 1867:

"For successive years the deaf mutes of the Commonwealth through annual appropriations have been placed for instruction and training in the asylum at Hartford. While, in the treatment of these unfortunates, science was at fault and methods were crude, in the absence of local provisions, this course was perhaps justifiable; but with added light of study and experience, which has explored the hidden ways and developed the mysterious laws by which the recesses of nature are reached, I cannot longer concur in the policy of expatriation, for I confess I share the sympathetic yearnings of the people of Massachusetts towards these children of the State detained by indissoluble chains in the domain of silence. This rigid grasp we may never relax, but over unseen waves, through the seemingly impassable gulf that separates them from their fellows, we may impart no small amount of abstract knowledge and moral culture. They are the wards of the State. Then, as ours is the responsibility, be ours also the grateful labor, and I know not to what supervision we may more safely intrust the delicate and intricate task than to the matured experience which has overcome the greater difficulty of blindness superadded to privation of speech and hearing. In no other object of philanthropy the warm heart of Massachusetts responds more promptly. Assured as I am on substantial grounds that legislative action in this direction will develop rich sources of private beneficence, I have the honor to recommend that the initial steps be taken to provide for this class of dependents within our own Commonwealth."

This portion of the Governor's message was referred to a large joint special committee, of which Mr. F. B. Fay was chairman on the part of the Senate, and Mr. J. L. Dudley on the part of the House. They did not limit their inquiries to the expediency of educating the deaf within the State, but spent much time in the investigation of the systems, and visited the American Asylum and the school of Miss Rogers at Chelmsford. They entered upon the inquiry almost entirely unacquainted with the methods of deaf mute education, and therefore comparatively free from predilections.

Dr. Howe and Mr. Sanborn, of the Board of State Charities ; Hon. Thomas Talbot, Mr. Hubbard, Mr.

Smith, of Boston, and a large number of deaf mutes from Boston and its vicinity favored the Governor's recommendations. Rev. Collins Stone, the principal, and W. W. Turner, the former principal of the asylum at Hartford; Hon. Calvin Day, its vice-president, and Hon. H. A. Stevens, of Boston, opposed them.

In the Report of the Committee dated May 27, 1867, it is said, "The advocates of a change of the policy of the State sustain the German system of teaching by articulation, while the representatives of the Hartford Asylum adhere to the French system of manual signs and finger-language." * * * "There is a radical difference of opinion in regard to the two systems entertained by those throughout the world who are most versed in the instruction of mutes." A short review of the arguments attached to their report makes this apparent. "The views of these gentlemen" (Dr. Howe, Mr. Sanborn, and Mr. Hubbard), said Mr. Stone, "are right in the teeth of the experience of all practical teachers. Every experiment that has been suggested has been tried and failed, and these are only the old questions over again." "If a child has lost his articulation entirely, and cannot hear at all, we hold that there is a better way of teaching him than by trying to teach him to talk." "Their recovery of articulation costs more than it is worth." "We do not give specific instruction in articulation; we consider it very much more efficient to throw our pupils on their articulation, in their daily intercourse with the teacher and the family. There was formerly a special instructor for these children, now there is none." "Where articulation is the method of instruction, religious worship is utterly impossible; I do not say religious *instruction* is impossible, but religious worship is out of the question. The world has never seen an instance where a person could stand up and speak to thirty or forty deaf mutes so that they would understand him. It is utterly out of the question. Mr. Turner said, "The attempt to teach articulation has never been a part of the regular system of instruction and I hope never will be, for I am firmly convinced that it is a comparatively useless branch." "We employed an especial teacher for eight or ten years, and prosecuted the work the whole of that time." "We never got them to speak off sentences." "We came to the conclusion after following that course for some ten years, that with the exception of these semi-mutes, who could speak pretty well when they came to us, our efforts accomplished very little."

Dr. Howe, in behalf of the "Board of Charities," urged the entire "abolition of the practice of expatriation, and called for the home education of our mutes, saying nothing at all about the system by which they were to be taught." He said: "I put it to any member of the Committee whether it is not better, if his child has any peculiarities that distinguish it, that he should take every possible measure to keep them out of sight even of the child itself, and bring the child under ordinary influences of society, so that when it comes into society, it shall not have anything peculiar. A little reflection will show that the aggregation of these persons together does increase these peculiarities."

Mr. Hubbard asked for a charter for the establishment of one or more schools, ''where semi-mute and semi-deaf and those congenital deaf mute children whose parents may desire to attempt their instruction in articulation may be taught,'' and ''where the education of the deaf might be commenced at an earlier age and continued for a longer period than at Hartford,'' and also for an appropriation in aid of the school.

Mr. Hubbard said: ''Watching the progress made by my own little girl, I have become interested in the subject of the teaching of deaf-mutes, and have paid some attention to that question of late years.

The views that I have been led to adopt from watching my own child and watching the progress made in this school, are these:—

1. That some deaf-mutes can be taught to articulate who are congenitally deaf; that is, those who have never heard.

2. That those who at an early period have lost their faculty of speech can be taught to articulate.

3. That those who preserve some portion of their hearing can also be taught to articulate.

4. That all, without great difficulty, can be taught to read from the lips.

It does not require any particular art or skill in the teacher to instruct deaf mutes. That I know of my own knowledge. It requires patience and constant application, and I know this too, from the education of my own child, that the more that child is brought into connection with other children that talk and articulate, the greater is her progress. And my belief is that if she had to be in an asylum with deaf mutes, she would soon lose all her faculty of articulation and of reading from the lips. She now plays with all the little girls, and goes to dancing school, and, after a little while, it is our intention to send her to other schools with other children. I have thus stated that there were three classes of deaf mutes who could be, in my opinion, taught this method of articulation. These three classes embrace, I believe, from one-half to three-fourths of the entire number of deaf mutes in the Commonwealth ; so that there are, therefore, a large number who could be reached by this peculiar method of teaching articulation. And it has, therefore, seemed to me that it was a plan which was to be thoroughly tried by this State, that we might see whether articulation could not be taught to these three classes. I think, from my own observation, that the two methods of instruction,—that is, by the use of signs and by articulation,—cannot be carried on together. One must be taught to the exclusion of the other. Therefore it is not well to send a child who can talk, or who can hear, to the school at Hartford, where the sign language chiefly is used to communicate instruction.

What definite, what practical plan do we propose for the education of deaf mutes ? It is this, gentlemen. That you shall give to some gentleman, who will make the necessary application, a charter for the purpose of establishing one or more schools in this State for the instruction of deaf mutes. That charter being granted, we propose to ask that the State shall make the same appropriation to scholars who may desire to go to these schools that they do to those that go to Hartford. We do not wish to begin on any great scale. We have no objection to having the age limited at first to those from five to ten years. We propose to continue the school now at Chelmsford, where semi-mutes and semi-deaf people, and those congenital deaf-mute children whose parents may desire to attempt their instruction in articulation, may be sent. Then we propose to open another school at Boston, where other deaf mutes may be taught, perhaps by the language of signs (for we will not object to using any system by which we can teach the deaf mutes, although I do not myself believe in the language of signs), but using more the manual alphabet than signs. Then we propose to establish another school, if you please, in Northampton. Beginning in a small, humble way, we wish to see if we cannot teach these semi-mutes; if we cannot by beginning at the early age of five years, restore articulation to those who have lost it and fit them for some higher school—fit them, if you please, for Hartford—but, at any rate, preserve for these young semi-mutes their powers of articulation.

This, gentlemen, is the general view which we have taken of the subject. We are here on our own behalf, without any connection in this matter with Dr. Howe or with the State Board of Charities.

Mr. DUDLEY. Would you not consider it a great gain, if the question of articulation were to be waived at the start, to have provision made for pupils between the ages of five and ten, leaving it to men not committed either way to determine the method of instruction ? Do we not want such a school, whatever the method of instruction may be?

Mr. HUBBARD. I have no doubt that would be a great gain. I think that was what I stated. We have one school at Chelmsford where they may be taught articulation. That is to be continued. It makes no difference whether the State helps it or not, that school is going on ; the experiment is to be tried of teaching semi-mutes articulation. When we were here two years ago, it was said to the Committee that there had been no attempt made to establish a school, that nothing had been done. Now we have got a school, and you are going to see it. That school is to be continued. But I am not wedded to the idea of teaching articulation to deaf mutes ; I doubt very much whether it can be taught to congenital deaf mutes ; but I do believe in teaching these young semi-mutes the English language. What do they seek to do at Hartford, and what do all who instruct pupils, whether deaf or not, attempt? It is to enable the pupils to communicate with others ; to elevate and improve them, and instruct them in language. They say that at Hartford they instruct their pupils in the natural language of signs.

Mr. STONE. Mr. Hubbard labors under a mistake. We do not instruct them in the natural language of signs, any more than you teach your child English when you use English to explain French. We make use of this natural language of the deaf and dumb child to teach him our language. We do not give our children instruction in the language of signs ; it is their vernacular language, and we take that language to instruct them in the English language.

Mr. HUBBARD: * * * They may not, perhaps, have any regular lessons in teaching sign language, as we did not give our little deaf child any lessons in articulation, or any lessons in reading upon the lips, and yet she is continually taught articulation by seeing us talk, by talking with us, by seeing the motion of our lips ; so their children are receiving, every day, instruction in the sign language, from the time they go until the time they leave the institution. When they go, as we have seen, they know nothing but natural signs; when they leave they are instructed in very many conventional signs. The pupils think in these signs.

* * * This language of signs, then, becomes their mother tongue ; it becomes their vernacular, as is said again and again in these reports.* The English

---

* My mother says :

The language used in institutions of the deaf is not the language of the hearing among whom they are to live. For developing the mental faculties, for enriching the mind with knowledge and thought the sign language may have been a success, but for fitting the deaf for daily intercourse with the hearing it has been an entire failure. The instruction of years has allowed and encouraged as a medium of thought and intercourse with his associates a language entirely unlanguage is to them like the French language, the Latin language, or the Greek language to the scholar at school.

This system of sign language, as it seems to us, tends to isolation and segregation. Dr. Stone has objected to that expression, and says that deafness is itself isolation. We agree that it is isolation; but the object of instructing deaf mutes is to bring them into communion with the outside world. The instruction at Hartford does it to a considerable extent, but not to so great an extent, we think, as teaching ought. We say that even here in Boston, the natural tendency of the deaf mutes is to segregation—to forming a community by themselves. As we are told in one of the New York reports, the instructed deaf mutes, if they could have their own way, would form a colony by themselves. This system of teaching deaf mutes the English language through signs seems to us very much like undertaking to teach, if you please, a Greenlander or a Sandwich Islander, who is to live all the time where the English language is spoken, the English language through the Greenland or Sandwich Island

---

intelligible to those among whom he must live his life after he leaves the Institution. It is too late for him to learn *their* language. A few—when we recall the herculean task described by Mr. Turner—how few—may learn *his* language, but he must ever be lonely and alone. "Nature made me deaf but man kept me dumb" was the remark made by a deaf mute. "Why was I not taught to speak?" was the expression of a longing for something better than the sign language from one who had tested it a life long under the most favoring circumstances. Why?—because neither husband nor son believed in the practicability of teaching speech to the deaf.

language. In order to teach him in that way, you must in the first place build up the Greenland language by new words introduced into it, and then, through this as a medium, teach him the English language. Why not teach him the English language at once, instead of going through this difficult process? Why not teach these deaf mutes at once the English language, rather than teach them by these signs?

But, gentlemen, great good has been done to the deaf mutes at Hartford ; great good is still done. The simple question is, Is there any other feasible method of instruction? Is there any improvement upon it?

The deaf mutes of Boston and vicinity were present at every hearing of the Committee and passed resolutions at the meeting of their association, which were read by Mr. Sanborn, urging the early education of the deaf, and within the State.

The Committee, May 27, 1867, recommended the passage of two bills which they reported. The first bill provided for the incorporation of the Clarke Institution for Deaf Mutes at Northampton, with authority to establish classes for instruction in two other suitable localities.

The others provided :

1st. For the education of certain deaf children between five and ten years of age by the Clarke Institution at the expense of the Commonwealth.

2nd. For extending the time devoted to the instruction of deaf children from six to ten years.

3rd. For the supervision, by the Board of Education, of the instruction of all deaf mute pupils aided by the Commonwealth.

4th. For an additional appropriation to carry out these objects

The report was opposed by two leading members of the House, Mr. R. H. Dana, whose wife was from Hartford, and Mr. Jewell, whose family lived in that city. The result was doubtful, when Mr. Dudley* arose, described and contrasted the condition of his daughter and my daughter, the pleasure and profits derived from speech, and the advantages of the oral system. His speech was most effective. The opposition was silenced and the bill passed almost unanimously and was approved on the first day of June, 1867.

Thus was the Clarke Institution incorporated. Mr. Clarke, whose modesty was as great as his generosity, was unwilling to have the Institution called by his name, and it was only after repeated solicitations that he consented, in deference to the wishes of his friends.

The corporation was organized on the 15th day of July, 1867. A committee waited upon Mr. Clarke with a copy of the Act of Incorporation and of the By-Laws. They returned in a few moments and reported that Mr. Clarke was ready that very morn-

---

*I remember Mr. Dudley's asking me during this hearing: "Do you think, Mr. Hubbard, that Theresa can ever be taught to say father and mother?" When two years after we heard her prattling without confining herself to those two words, I reminded him of the conversation.

ing to transfer to the institution forty thousand dollars in government securities at the market price in New York, and an additional amount sufficient to make the sum of $50,000 when required by the Corporation. The balance was paid within the year, and an additional legacy of $200,000 was left in his will. This is believed to be the largest donation ever made in this country by an individual to an institution for the benefit of deaf-mutes.

The corporators, at the time of its organization, were not pledged to any system of instruction, and the majority of them had no decided opinion upon the subject; but at the first meeting the question was practically decided by the adoption of the report of the School Committee, which recommended, among other things, that "an articulating school, under the charge of Miss Rogers, be established at Northampton."

The school of Miss Rogers was moved from Chelmsford to Northampton, and formed the nucleus of the Clarke Institution. The basis on which it is conducted is clearly expressed in the first report:

"There are various classes of deaf-mutes who can be taught by articulation. These are:

A. Those who lost their hearing at three years of age and upwards, after they acquired some language which they retain.

B. Those congenitally deaf who have good mental ability and a capacity for learning to speak.

C. Those who are semi-deaf and can distinguish articulate sounds, but not really enough to attend the common school with profit."

It was also decided that it should be a family and home school, and the influence of home be secured for the pupils, not alone in school hours, but on the play ground and at meals, attendants always being with the children at their play and teachers sitting at table with their pupils. This home influence and constant contact of the teachers with the pupils has been one of the chief causes which has enabled us to achieve, to so large an extent, the object we sought.

The School opened on October 1st, 1867. We knew little of the German method of instruction. Miss Rogers knew only the fact that in Germany the deaf were taught by articulation. She, however, and her successor, Miss Yale, have from time to time tried various methods of teaching the deaf to speak and read from the lips. They have visited the European schools and have studied the methods employed in them, and they have at last made this school one of the best of its kind in the world. Though at first we thought it would be hardly possible to teach the congenitally deaf to speak and read from the lips, yet we soon found that they could be taught and the record of the very first year shows, that, of the twenty pupils, eleven, or a majority, whether either congenitally deaf or had lost their hearing at two years or under, and before they had acquired any language. The number of such pupils taught in our school has been continually increasing, and now over seventy per cent. are of that class. They are no longer dumb, for the pupils we have graduated have gone into the world speaking men and women.

Our institution from the very first year has been visited by the principals and teachers of schools in different parts of the country, who have come to observe our methods of instruction, and thus a knowledge of our methods has been carried far and wide. In the third annual report it is recorded that teachers from the Ohio and Illinois institutions had spent some time in Northampton and that classes in articulation and lip reading had been organized in the State Institutions of New York, Ohio, Illinois, Wisconsin and the American Asylum at Hartford.

Recalling what Mr. Turner so positively stated before the Committee in 1867, that when articulation was the method employed, religious worship with thirty or forty deaf persons in attendance was an impossibility, it is interesting to copy from the reports of the Clarke School for 1874 and 1875.

"All the older pupils, numbering twenty or thirty, gather every morning in the chapel, where a short passage of the Scriptures is explained and applied, followed by *extempore* prayer. With the younger pupils there is a shorter and simpler devotional worship. The services commence with the reading of a portion of the beautiful liturgy of the Episcopal Church. All rise and repeat the selection aloud; hymns are read and repeated in the same way, from a collection prepared for the purpose. Then the little congregation is addressed by the teacher. Seated before her, every eye intent upon her face, these young souls receive through her the lessons of a Father's kindness and a Savior's love. Literally from her lips comes the message of love and redemption. She speaks precisely as she would had all present the ability of hearing possessed by herself. Yet these pupils understand the message and there is true, though, to them, silent worship."

In 1892 the Clarke Institution celebrated the twenty-fifth anniversary of its founding, and welcomed within its walls representatives from sister institutions. Among them were the principal and teachers of the American Asylum, of the Philadelphia Institution, and Mr. F. B. Sanborn, its staunch friend from the beginning.

The Superintendent of the Pennsylvania Institution, Dr. Crouter, in his address, said :—

"The influence of the Clarke Institution in shaping methods of instructing the deaf has been potent, more potent, in my opinion, than any other school in the country. Her influence has been more potent than even that of old Hartford, whose work we all so greatly admire, for Hartford wrought in virgin soil, while Clarke has been compelled to work in the face of adverse conditions, against prejudice and established methods."

Mr. Sanborn said :—

"It is worthy of note that France itself, where the Abbé de l'Epée in the last century so intelligently and generously established instruction by signs, has long since adopted in its national institutions the oral method ; which there had to overcome, not only the traditions we have encountered in this country, but also the natural aversion of the French towards adopting any system that could be described as German. In fact, the oral method, however, is neither German, nor English, nor Dutch, nor even Spanish,* but is the natural method, to which other systems must in time give way, however ingenious and useful they may have proved to be."

One of the first results of the discussions at the hearings before the committee in 1867 was the founding of the Horace Mann School for the Deaf in Boston. Rev. Dexter S. King, a member of that committee and also a member of the school committee of Boston, had taken an especial interest in the hearings. He attended every meeting, visited our little school at Chelmsford, called repeatedly to see my daughter, and aided us by every means in his power to obtain our charter, having first inserted a provision giving us a right to establish schools in two other suitable places besides Northampton. Mr. King's interest in the education of deaf children, instead of decreasing with the granting of our charter, increased.

Scarcely was the Clarke School opened when he asked that a branch might be started in Boston. This being impossible, Mr. King, as a member of the school board, secured the appointment of a committee to consider this subject in 1868 and 1869. The school was opened in November, 1869, as an articulation school under the name of School for Deaf Mutes, with Miss Sarah Fuller as principal. She

* Mr. Sanborn here refers to the fact that the first systematic efforts at teaching the deaf were made in Spain by Bonet. His method was articulation, and was so successful as to excite the notice of the suite of the Prince of Wales, afterwards Charles I, who was visiting Spain in search of a wife.

had been a public school teacher and fitted herself for her new work for the deaf by study at Northampton. It was, with the exception of a sign school at Pittsburg, which antedated it by six weeks, the first day school for the deaf in this country and was the first in teaching by the new method. The Pittsburg managers had, however, no real faith in the principle of day schools, and in 1876 their school became an institution, or boarding school.

The Boston School, soon renamed the "Horace Mann School for the Deaf," therefore stands for a new departure in the education of the deaf. Before this they had been gathered into institutions, apart from friends, isolated from the world around them, a distinct and separate community. This plan was then thought necessary to their education. Institutions for the deaf are undoubtedly necessary in every State, as children must be gathered from distant points; but wherever there are in cities a sufficient number of children, day schools are certainly to be preferred. The home influence, the strong ties of affection, are often more important to the deaf child than to the hearing; for he is less prepared to fight the battle of life. The Horace Mann School has proved by its continued and growing success that to deaf as well as to others all the advantages of school education can be extended without the severance of home and family ties. As the direct offspring of this, the first day school, similar schools have grown up in other States and its influence is felt through the length and breadth of the land.

The success of our schools in which we rejoice is due not only to the superiority of the oral system over the sign language system, not only to the energy and perseverence of the founders, but more than all to the devotion, to the untiring zeal, and to the ability of our teachers. No other teaching is so exacting, requires such constant attention and unwearied application. The names of all these teachers are too numerous to mention. In our earthly as in our heavenly firmament one star differeth from another in glory, but bright as constellations shine the names of Miss Rogers and Miss Yale, Miss Fuller and Miss Bond.

In England, as well as in our own country, the influence of our work has been felt. In 1871, an English gentleman, Mr. B. St. John Ackers, visited the various schools of England and America seeking for the best means of educating his own deaf child. He decided that she should be taught by articulation, rather than by signs, which was the system then used in the English institutions. He was so much pleased with the Horace Mann school that he engaged one of its teachers, Miss Barton, to return with him. More and more convinced of the superiority of "articulation teaching," and feeling the importance of thorough and earnest teachers, he was led to establish a normal school, which has sent out many teachers well fitted for their work. Subsequently, Mr. Ackers, then a member of Parliament, was influential in securing the appointment of a "Royal Commission" to investigate and report upon the condition of the blind, the deaf, and the dumb of the United Kingdom, and was appointed one of the Commission by the Queen.

In their report the Commission recommended:

"That every child who is deaf should have full opportunity of education in the oral system; that all children should be, for the first year at least, instructed in the oral system and after the first year they should be taught to speak and lip-read on the oral system unless they were physically deficient.

"That children who had partial hearing should in all cases be instructed in the pure oral system.

"That trained teachers of the deaf should, as in Germany, receive salaries such as would induce teachers of special attainments to enter the profession, and on a higher scale than those enjoyed by trained teachers of ordinary children."

When we consider that the interest in deaf mute education which formed the Royal Commission, and that its recommendations which have so changed the system of education in Great Britain, have been a direct outgrowth from our work, have we not reason to believe that the seed sown in our weakness has already borne much fruit and will yield a still more abundant harvest? Have we not reason to be glad of the past and to take courage for the future?

Twenty years ago I stated to the Legislature of Massachusetts that there were many semi-mutes who had lost their hearing at an early age, who retained much language and who could be taught speech and lip-reading, possibly fifty per cent. in all, who could be taught by the oral method. With greater confidence I say now that when the next twenty-five years have rolled around and when the Clarke Institution shall hold its jubilee, then it will be found that not fifty per cent., but that every deaf and dumb child of unimpaired mental power, where-ever he may be, will be taught by the oral method alone and fitted to enter into the work of his country.

Believing then that for the deaf our system lessens their privations, brings them more into communication with their friends and fellows, and, instead of building up still higher the separating wall of a different language, opens to them as to others the treasures of written language, shall we not rejoice that it has been our privilege to work to this end, and that out of the affliction of a little child a blessing has come to many?